FJ

D0231467

70001671623 3

BEEP BEEP BEEP TIME FOR SLEEP!

For Thomas and Luke, the lovely
grandsons of Nannie Rose xx – CF

To my wife, for all your patience
and encouragement – RS

Haringey Libraries	
FF	
Askews & Holts	17-Feb-2016
JF	
	HAJR3/11/15

SIMON AND SCHUSTER
First published in Great Britain in 2016 by Simon and Schuster UK Ltd • 1st Floor, 222 Gray's Inn Road, London WC1X 8HB
A CBS Company • Text copyright © 2016 Claire Freedman • Illustrations copyright © 2016 Richard Smythe • The right of
Claire Freedman and Richard Smythe to be identified as the author and illustrator of this work has been asserted by them in
accordance with the Copyright, Designs and Patents Act, 1988 • All rights reserved, including the right of reproduction in
whole or in part in any form • A CIP catalogue record for this book is available from the British Library upon request
ISBN: 978-1-4711-2114-2 (PB) • eBook ISBN: 978-1-4711-2115-9 (eBook) • Printed in China • 10 9 8 7 6 5 4 3 2 1

BEEP BEEP BEEP
TIME FOR SLEEP!

Claire Freedman & Richard Smythe

SIMON AND SCHUSTER

London New York Sydney Toronto New Delhi

It's been a busy working day,
road building on the motorway.

Vroooom!

Heavy lorries thunder past.

Swish!

Vans and cars, all driving fast!

Backhoe loader
jolts and **judders.**
When he drills the whole road
shudders!

Digger's sharp teeth hit the earth.
He's **clawing** holes for all he's worth.

Reversing warning!

Beep! Beep! Beep!

Here's tipper truck
with one more heap.

Dusty dump truck at the double,
tips his load of **stones**
and

rubble.

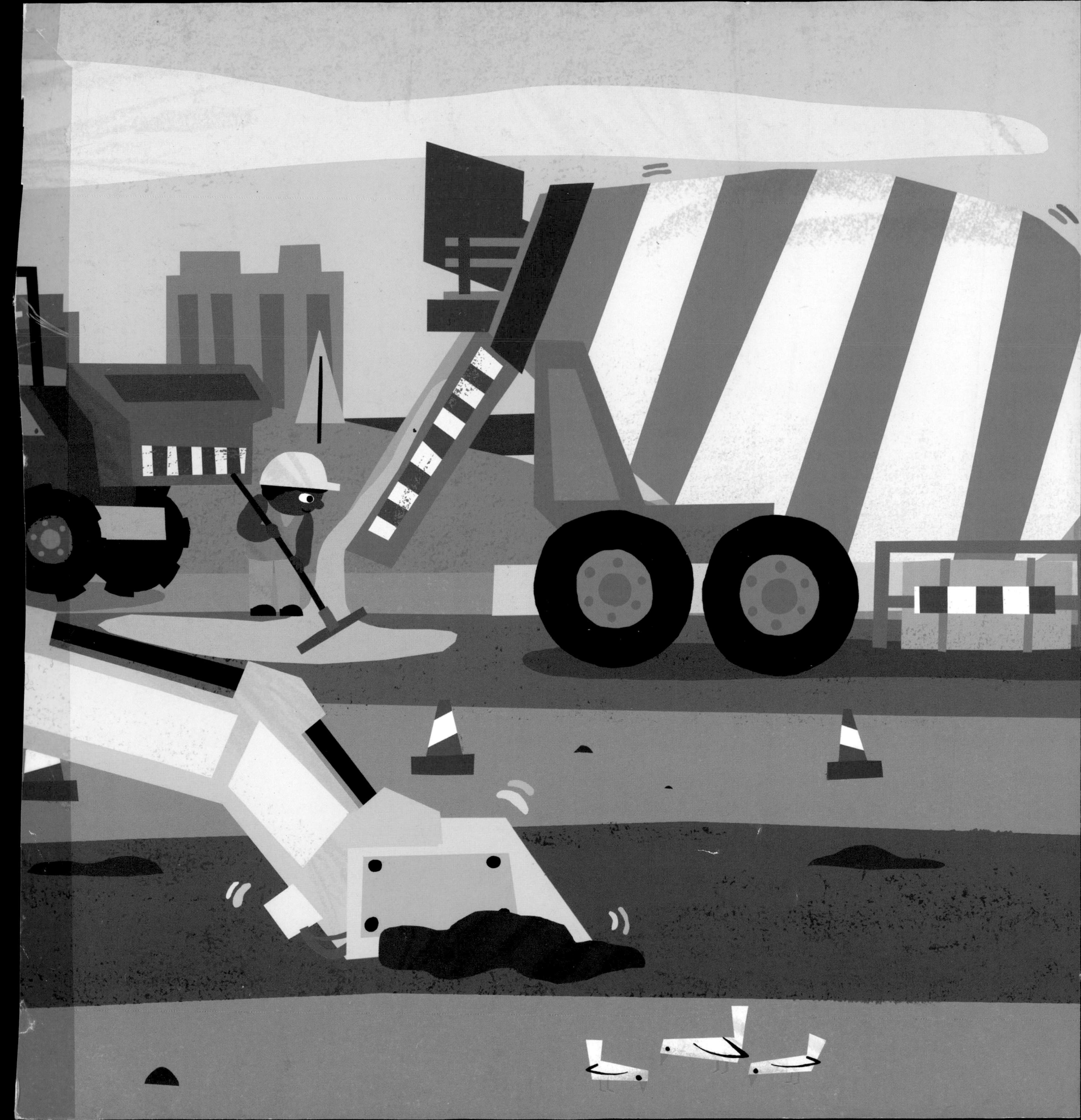

Concrete mixer's drum is turning —
sand, cement and
gravel churning.

Grader, with his giant blade,
soon gets the sticky asphalt laid.

Then huge road roller, with a **clatter**,
loves to press the tarmac flatter.

But quiet now it's getting late
and digging roads will have to wait.

Backhoe loader, stop your **drill.**
The sun has sunk behind the hill.

Time to wind down, time for stopping.

Hear concrete mixer's engine **popping!**

Shadows fall, the work day ends
for all the roadwork building friends.

New road signs flash up overhead,
please take the slip road off to **bed.**

After tipper's rough tough day, he's hosed down with a **cooling spray.**

Clean up digger – no more rush!
His giant bucket gets a brush.

Tired road roller's done his best,
it's time to **stop,** it's time to **rest.**

Dump truck parks up for the night.

He cuts his motor, **dims** his light.

Grader yawns and off he lumbers,
soon to snore in
sleepy slumbers.

Traffic cones light up his way,
shimmering in the dusky grey.

All tucked up safely in their yard,
they snuggle down, they've worked so hard.
Soon **sparkling stars** begin to peep
as one by one they fall asleep.

The silver moonlight softly gleams.

Goodnight big machines, sweet dreams!